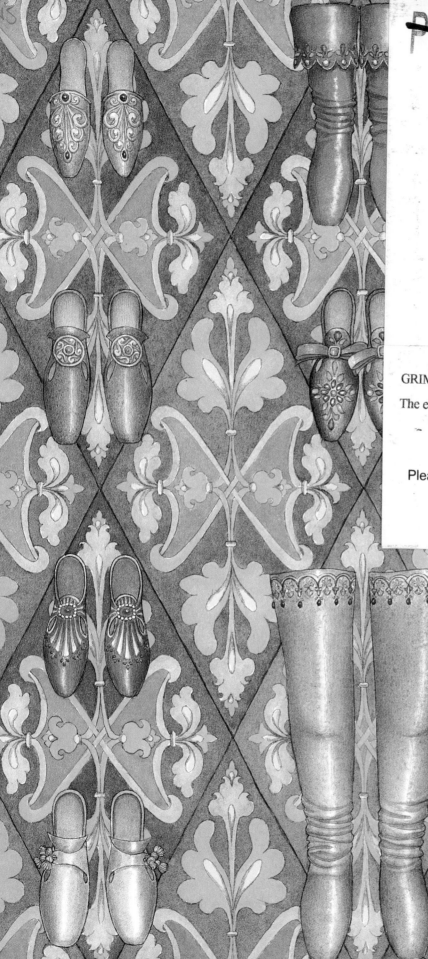

THE
ELVES
AND THE
SHOEMAKER

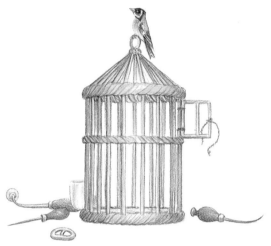

Barefoot Books Ltd
PO Box 95
Kingswood
Bristol
BS30 5BH

This book has been printed on 100% acid-free paper

Graphic design by Jennie Hoare
Colour reproduction by Grafiscan, Verona
Printed and bound in Singapore by Tien Wah Press (Pte) Ltd

Hardback ISBN 1 901223 72 8
Paperback ISBN 1 902283 06 6

British Library Cataloguing-in-Publication Data:
a catalogue record for this book is available from the British Library

1 3 5 7 9 8 6 4 2

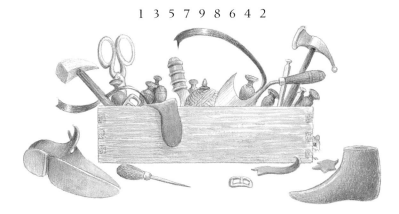

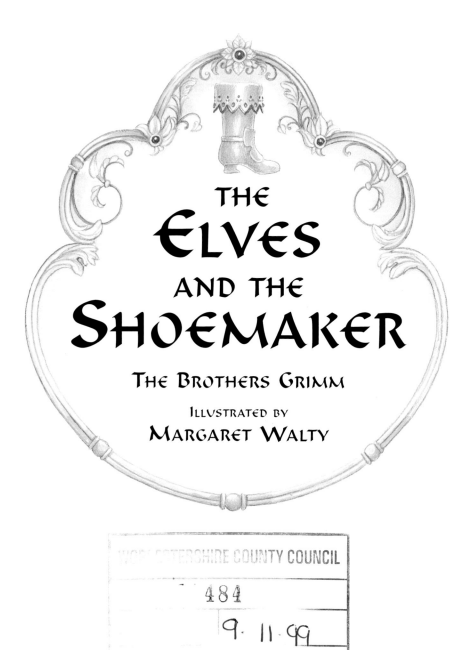

THE
ELVES
AND THE
SHOEMAKER

THE BROTHERS GRIMM

ILLUSTRATED BY
MARGARET WALTY

BAREFOOT BOOKS
BATH

LONG AGO, a young shoemaker and his wife lived together in a beautiful city. The shoemaker worked hard all day and was very honest with all of his customers; but no matter how many shoes he made, he could not earn enough money for him and his wife to live upon. Finally, the day came when all that he had left in his workshop was one small piece of leather.

That evening, the shoemaker
quietly and carefully cut out the
piece of leather to make his last pair
of shoes the following morning. He
and his wife had no food to eat, so
they went to bed hungry. But, in
spite of their troubles, they still felt
thankful that they had each other,
and soon they fell into a deep and
peaceful sleep.

The next morning, the shoemaker
and his wife woke up early. Without
wasting a moment, the shoemaker
went downstairs to do his work.
To his astonishment, there on his
worktable stood a fine pair of shoes,
ready made!

The shoemaker called out to his wife, and for a long time both of them gazed in amazement at the new pair of shoes.

The shoemaker picked up each one in turn and inspected it carefully. There was not one false stitch in the whole job; they were the most exquisite pair of shoes he had ever seen.

That morning, a very rich man was walking through the town with his wife when he noticed the shoes on display in the workshop. The shoes suited him so well that he willingly offered the shoemaker a very high price for them. With the money, the shoemaker's wife was able to go out shopping and buy enough food to cook a delicious dinner. She also bought enough leather for her husband to make two more pairs of shoes. In the evening, the shoemaker cut out the leather once more, laid out the pieces on his worktable and went to bed early.

But once again, the shoemaker was
saved the trouble of having to make up
the shoes, for in the morning he found
both pairs sitting on his worktable,
with not a stitch out of place. Soon two
customers arrived, and they paid him
handsomely, for they had never seen
such fine shoes.

Now the shoemaker's wife could
buy enough food to cook dinner
and enough leather for four new
pairs of shoes.

After the couple had eaten, the
shoemaker cut out the leather
again and left it on his worktable.
The same thing happened as had
happened before: during the night,
the leather that had been laid out
in the evening was made into four
perfect pairs of shoes.

And so it went on for some time;
what was ready in the evening was
always made into shoes by daybreak.
Before long, the shoemaker and his
wife had everything they needed.

One evening, just before Christmas,
as he and his wife were sitting by the
fire, the shoemaker said, 'I would like
to sit up and watch tonight, so that we
may see who it is that comes and does
my work for me.' 'What a good idea!'
exclaimed his wife. So they left a
candle burning and hid themselves
behind a curtain in a corner of
the room, and waited.

As soon as the town clock struck midnight, in came two little elves, quite naked. They sat themselves down on the shoe-maker's table, took up all the leather that was cut out, and set to work. They stitched and rapped and hammered and tapped faster than anyone the shoemaker had ever seen.

Within a few minutes the job was done, and a neat row of shoes stood ready for use upon the table. Then the two elves scurried away, as quickly and mysteriously as they had come.

While the couple were out walking together the next evening, the shoemaker's wife stopped outside a draper's shop and said, 'Those little elves have made us rich, and we ought to be thankful to them and do them a good turn if we can. I was quite sorry to see them going around with no clothes to keep them warm. Listen, I have an idea. I shall buy some scraps of fabric at this shop and make each of them a linen shirt, a silk waistcoat, and a velvet coat and pair of trousers into the bargain. You can make each of them a little pair of shoes.'

This idea pleased the shoemaker very much. So whenever they had a free moment, he and his wife worked on the elves' new outfits. At last, everything was ready. That evening, the couple laid the clothes out neatly on the table, instead of the usual pieces of leather. Then they lit a small candle and hid themselves once more behind the curtain.

As soon as the town clock struck
midnight, in danced the two elves.
When they saw the new clothes laid
out for them, they laughed out loud.
The shoemaker and his wife smiled
at each other. The elves dressed
themselves in the twinkling of an
eye. They danced and skipped and
capered all over the chairs and
tables, whooping and singing with
delight. And then, just as suddenly
as before, they were gone.

The shoemaker and his wife went happily to bed and slept peacefully. They never saw the two elves again. But they always remembered their midnight helpers, and everything went well with them from that time forward. Over the years they had many children, and there was nothing the children liked to hear more than the magical story of the two little elves.

THE END

BAREFOOT BOOKS publishes high-quality picture books for children of all ages and specialises in the work of artists and writers from many cultures. If you have enjoyed this book and would like to receive a copy of our current catalogue, please contact our London office — tel: 0171 704 6492 fax: 0171 359 5798   email: sales@barefoot-books.com website: www.barefoot-books.com